# What's the difference?
# Fish

## Stephen Savage

RSVP
RAINTREE
STECK-VAUGHN
PUBLISHERS
A Steck-Vaughn Company
Austin, Texas
www.steck-vaughn.com

# What's the difference?

# Amphibians Insects
# Birds Mammals
# Fish Reptiles

**Cover:** The great white shark and a goldfish

**Title page:** A mudskipper and (inset) sea horses

**Contents page:** A giant gourami

Published by Raintree Steck-Vaughn Publishers, an imprint of Steck-Vaughn Company

Printed in Italy. Bound in the United States.
1 2 3 4 5 6 7 8 9 0 03 02 01 00 99

**Library of Congress Cataloging-in-Publication Data**
Savage, Stephen.
Fish / Stephen Savage.
    p.   cm.—(What's the difference)
    Includes bibliographical references and index.
    Summary: Describes the physical characteristics common to all fish and highlights the differences between various species, including habitats, methods of moving around, feeding habits, and raising their young.
    ISBN 0-7398-1357-9 (hard)
    0-7398-1821-X (soft)
    1. Fishes—Juvenile literature.
    [1. Fishes.]
    I. Title.  II. Series.
    QL617.2.S29  2000
    597—dc21          99-16014

# Contents

# What a Difference!

There are about 22,000 different types of fish. They come in all sizes, shapes, and colors.

Although a goldfish looks very different from a shark, both are types of fish. They have some of the same basic features.

▼ The whale shark is about 60 ft. (18 m) long and is the largest fish in the world. It eats small fish and plankton, sucking them into its enormous mouth.

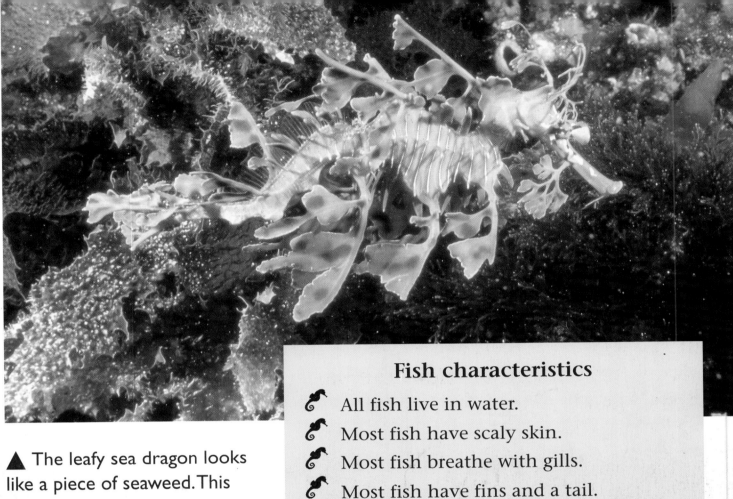

▲ The leafy sea dragon looks like a piece of seaweed. This camouflage helps protect it from attack.

## Fish characteristics

🐟 All fish live in water.

🐟 Most fish have scaly skin.

🐟 Most fish breathe with gills.

🐟 Most fish have fins and a tail.

🐟 Most fish have a swim bladder to help them float.

## Simple key to the Animal Kingdom

```
                    Simple key to the Animal Kingdom
                                   |
            ┌──────────────────────┴──────────────────────┐
      Invertebrates                                  Vertebrates
    ┌────────┬────────┐                      ┌────────┬────────┬────────┐
  Worms            Spiders                   Fish         Reptiles   Mammals
        Snails          Insects        Amphibians      Birds
```

An invertebrate is an animal that does not have a backbone.

A vertebrate is an animal that has a backbone.

# Where Fish Live

About two thirds of the earth's surface is covered by water. Fish live in all the world's seas and oceans. Their habitats include the sandy seabed, coral reefs, and underwater forests.

## Fish and different habitats

- Saltwater fish cannot live in fresh water.
- Freshwater fish cannot live in salt water.
- A few types of fish can live in both fresh and salt water.
- Flatfish have flat bodies, so they can rest on the seabed.

▼ Piranhas swim in large schools in South American rivers. They have very sharp teeth for eating other fish and occasionally large mammals.

Fish also live in tropical rivers, cool lakes, and icy mountain streams. They can live almost anyplace where there is water.

▲ This peacock grouper lives mainly on coral reefs. It lies in wait for smaller fish, which it swallows whole.

◄ Angler fish live in deep parts of the oceans. They have a long, shiny nose-type feature that attracts smaller fish in the dark ocean depths.

# Catching a Meal

The shape of a fish's mouth gives a clue to the type of food it eats. Predators, like sharks and piranhas, have large mouths filled with pointed teeth.

◀ The great white shark has large, pointed teeth. Each tooth is about 3 in. (7.5 cm) long. It eats the flesh of anything from fish to sea lions.

▼ This butterfly fish has a long, thin snout for catching food hiding in small cracks and among coral.

Fish that eat tiny sea creatures have a small mouth suitable for snapping up their food. Others, like the queen trigger fish, have sharp, chisel-like teeth to open the hard bodies of shellfish.

▲ The puffer fish inflates itself so that it appears too large for predators to eat.

◀ Catfish use their sensitive "whiskers" to find food. They eat mainly other fish.

Some fish feed by sucking up large mouthfuls of mud from the river bottom. They swallow the tiny creatures hiding in the mud and spit the rest out.

A few types of fish bury themselves in the sand on the seabed. They grab and eat any fish that gets too close.

### Fish defenses

- Most fish live in large schools, or groups, which helps protect them.
- Some fish have false eye spots to trick predators.
- Many fish are colored so that they blend into their surroundings.
- Some fish have poisonous spines.

▼ The lionfish is brightly colored, which warns other animals that it is poisonous.

▼ This archer fish is spitting water at an insect to knock it into the water from an overhanging leaf.

# Hot and Cold

Fish live in oceans or rivers that are warm, cool, or cold. A fish that is used to living in a warm sea would die in a cold sea.

◀ This lungfish will survive even when there is no water in the river. (Above) When the river dries up, it will burrow into the mud, breathing with special lungs.

▲ A few types of fish live in pools that dry up in the dry season. This gardner's killifish may die, but its eggs will live and hatch when it rains again. (Inset) Killifish eggs hatching in a rain-filled pool

A few types of fish live in some of the hottest and driest parts of the world. For some months of the year, there is no water at all.

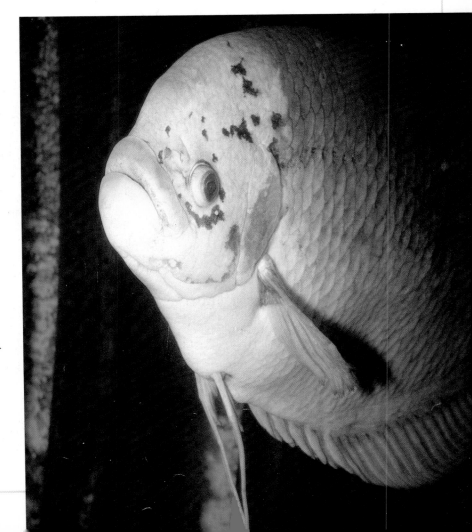

The giant gourami lives in warm ▶ water, which has less oxygen than cooler water. It survives by gulping air at the surface, using a special lung.

In the winter, when rivers and lakes become cold, fish rest near the bottom and hardly move until the water is warmer.

▼ In the winter seashore fish like this common blenny may move to deeper water, which will be warmer.

## How fish cope in hot and cold conditions

🐟 Desert pupfish can live in water temperatures more than 100° F (50° C).

🐟 Antarctic fish live in water temperatures as low as 28° F (-2° C).

🐟 Some fish migrate to warmer climates.

▼ The icefish lives in the freezing waters of the Antarctic Ocean.

Fish living in Arctic and Antarctic waters can survive freezing temperatures. They produce a chemical that acts as an antifreeze to keep their blood from freezing.

# Getting Around

Most fish swim by moving their tails from side to side. The fins on the top and bottom of their bodies keep the fish upright.

▲ Rays have large, winglike fins. These eagle rays swim by using a graceful movement of their fins or by gliding.

The sailfish is the fastest swimming fish. It can swim at a speed of 68 mph (109 km/h).

A fish uses the fins on the side of its body to steer. The faster a fish moves its tail from side to side, the faster it can swim.

▼ The gurnard "walks" along the seabed on special feelers. It uses these feelers to find animals hiding under the sand.

Some fish hide in rocky holes during the day and come out at night to feed. Coral reefs and shipwrecks provide plenty of hiding places.

▼ The moray eel lives in a deep, rocky hole. It swims by rippling its long body.

## Moving about

- Fish swim by moving their tails from side to side.
- Flying fish move their tails 50 beats a second to leap out of the water.
- Sharks have no swim bladder and will sink if they stop swimming.
- Sea horses can hover in the water.

◀ Mudskippers live in mangrove swamps. At low tide they move around on the mud, using leglike fins.

A few fish move differently than other fish. This includes gliding and even climbing out of the water in search of food.

▲ To escape predators, flying fish leap out of the sea and glide 30 ft. (10 m) or more. The flying fish's side fins are like wings.

# Fish Young

Fish have developed different ways to make sure their young survive. Most fish lay eggs, but a few give birth to live young.

▼ Adult salmon live in the sea. To give birth, they return to the same river in which they hatched. There the female lays thousands of tiny eggs.

Most egg-laying fish lay thousands of eggs to make sure that some survive. Some sharks and rays lay fewer eggs, protected by a tough outer case. The young are larger than other newly hatched fish and are less likely to be eaten.

▲ The female guppy (bottom, below two males) has eggs that hatch inside her body. The young swim away as soon as they are born.

▼ You can see the baby dogfish growing inside these egg cases. The yolks provide food while they grow.

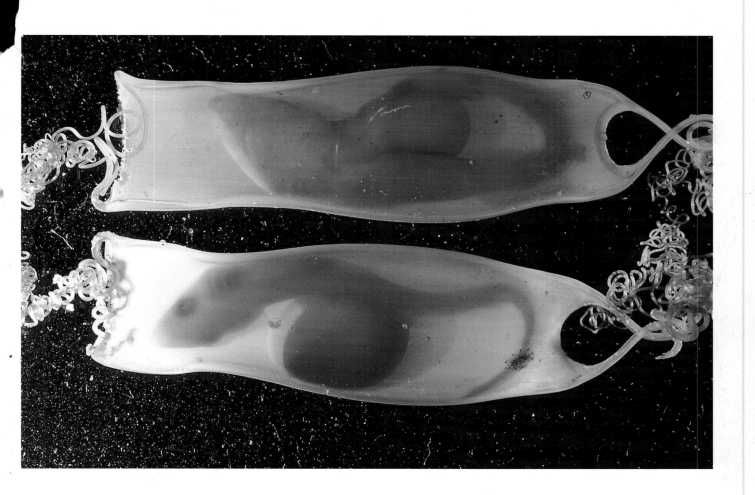

Some fish stay with their eggs and protect them against predators. They attack other fish that come too close.

A few types of fish lay their eggs in a nest. Other fish protect their eggs and young in more unusual ways.

▲ Male parent sea horses have a special pouch in which they keep the eggs until they are ready to hatch.

◀ The male Siamese fighting fish makes a nest by blowing a lot of bubbles. He collects the eggs laid by the female and blows them into the nest.

## Facts about eggs and young fish

🐚 A female sunfish lays 300 million eggs at one time, more than any other fish.

🐚 Some fish perform a courtship dance.

🐚 Male fish are often more colorful than females.

🐚 Some female wrasse can become males.

▼ Mouthbrooder cichlids carry their eggs in their mouth. The young fish return to the parent in times of danger.

# Fish Pets

People often keep fish as pets because of their fascinating shapes, colors, and movement. Sometimes they are kept in garden ponds.

◄ A goldfish has all the features of a typical fish, including a line of tiny holes along the side of its body that allow it to pick up vibrations.

Sticklebacks live ► in ponds and streams. They are sometimes caught and kept for a short time in a fish tank.

Fish can also be kept indoors in a fish tank. The tank should provide the same conditions for the fish as it would have in the wild.

▲ Some fish swim near the surface of ponds, while others live and feed near the bottom.

## How to care for your pet fish

🌊 Fish should be kept in a special fish tank. Some tanks have lids to protect the fish from harm.

🌊 Grow water plants in the tank and place rocks and sand in the bottom.

🌊 Feed your fish with the correct food.

🌊 Make sure the water is kept clean.

# Unusual Fish

▲ The lamprey has no jaws. It attaches itself to a large, bony fish with a sucker and feeds on its blood.

Most fish have a hard skeleton and bones. They are called "bony fish." Some fish, like sharks and rays, have softer skeletons.

## Strange facts

🐟 Although flatfish, such as sole and plaice, can lie flat on the seabed, they are hatched upright like other fish.

🐟 Cave fish live in dark caves and have no eyes.

🐟 The four-eyed fish can see predators above the water and food beneath the water at the same time.

Bony fish may have very unusual features, including a sucker for sticking to rocks or a body that looks like a rock. Some fish, like the cleaner wrasse, live with other fish in a way that helps both fish.

▲ Can you see the tiny fish in this larger fish's mouth? The tiny fish is called a cleaner wrasse. It lives with the larger fish, eating parasites that live on its body and cleaning it at the same time.

◄ The colorful boxfish has tiny fins on either side of its cube-shaped body.

# Scale of Fish

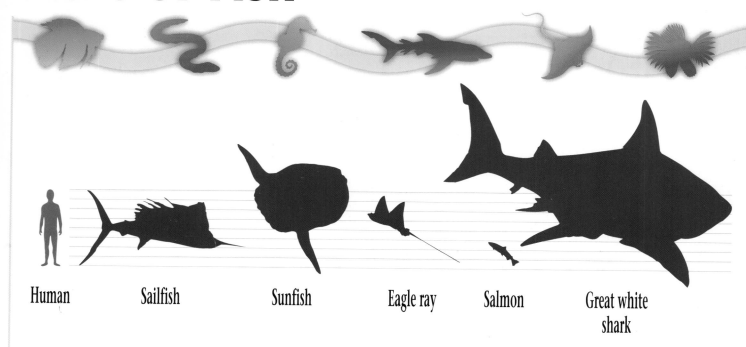

Human     Sailfish     Sunfish     Eagle ray     Salmon     Great white shark

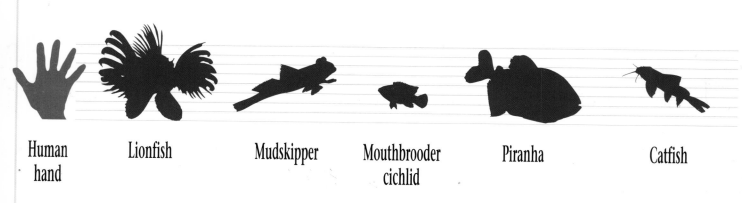

Human hand     Lionfish     Mudskipper     Mouthbrooder cichlid     Piranha     Catfish

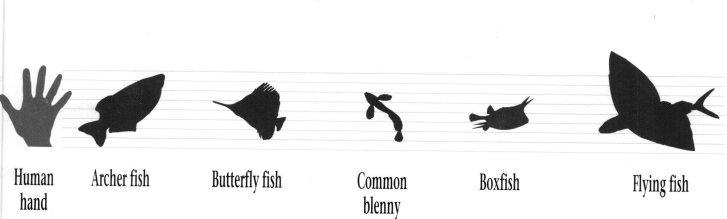

Human hand     Archer fish     Butterfly fish     Common blenny     Boxfish     Flying fish

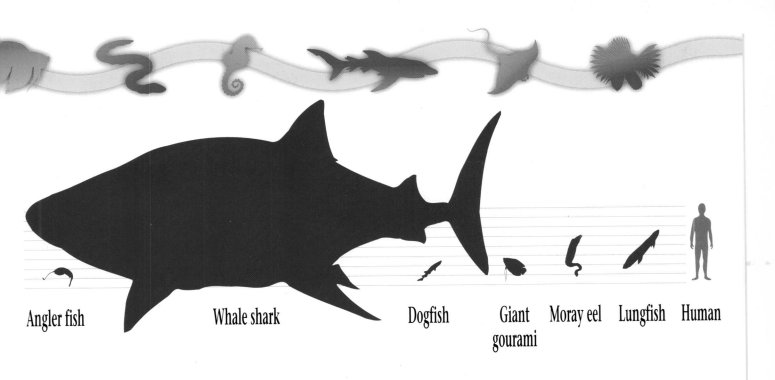

Angler fish       Whale shark       Dogfish       Giant gourami       Moray eel       Lungfish       Human

Peacock grouper       Puffer fish       Siamese fighting fish       Sea horse       3-spined stickleback       Cleaner wrasse       Human hand

Goldfish       Flying gurnard       Icefish       Killifish       Lamprey       Leafy sea dragon       Human hand

# Glossary

**Antarctic** The region at or around the South Pole.

**Arctic** The region at or around the North Pole.

**Camouflage** Protection from attack by appearing to be part of the surroundings.

**Coral reef** A ridge near the surface of the sea, formed in masses by the skeletons of tiny sea animals.

**Courtship dance** A dance performed to attract a mate.

**Habitats** The natural homes of plants and animals.

**Hatch** To produce young from eggs.

**Hover** To stay suspended, without moving forward.

**Mangrove swamp** An area covered with the roots of mangrove trees.

**Migrate** To move from one area to another to escape the cold.

**Parasites** Animals (or plants) that live and feed on others.

**Plankton** Minute animals and plants that are eaten by fish.

**Predators** Animals that hunt others for food.

**Schools** Groups of fish.

**Skeleton** The bony framework of the body of a fish and other animals.

**Sucker** An organ allowing an animal to cling to something by suction.

**Swim bladder** A gas-filled sac that helps a fish float and not sink.

**Tropical** To do with the tropics, the areas north and south of the equator.

**Vibrations** Tiny movements.

# Finding Out More

## Books to Read

Evans, Mark. *Fish*. New York: Dorling Kindersley, 1993.

Gallimard Jeunesse. *Fish*. New York: Scholastic, 1997.

Johnson, Jenny. *Children's Guide to Sea Creatures*. New York: Simon & Schuster Books for Young Adults, 1998.

Savage, Stephen. *Animals of the Oceans* (Animals by Habitat). Austin, TX: Raintree Steck-Vaughn, 1997.

## CD ROM

*Exploring Water Habitats* (Raintree Steck-Vaughn, 1997).

# Index

Page numbers in **bold** refer to photographs.

**Picture Acknowledgments:**

Bruce Coleman 8(l), 9, 16, /Franco Banfi 4, 7(t), /Luiz Claudio Marigo 6, /Hans Reinhard 10(t), 12(b), /Andrew Purcell 17(b), /C. Lockwood 18, /Jane Burton 19(t), 21, 24(b) and title page (inset), 25(t), /Hans Reinhard 26, /Bill Wood 27(b); FLPA /K. Aitken/Panda 5, /Frank Lane 13(b) and contents page, /D.P. Wilson 21(t), /Jeremy McCabe 23(t); NHPA /Norbert Wu 7(b), 8(r), /Trevor McDonald 10(b), /Stephen Dalton 11, /Daniel Heuclin 12(t), /Gerard Lacz 13(t), /14, /Laurie Campbell 15, Norbert Wu 17(t), 19(b), /B. & C. Alexander 20, /Jeff Foot Prod. 22 and title page, /Anthony Bannister 23(b), /B. Jonks & M. Shimlock 27(t); Oxford Scientific Films /Max Gibbs cover (inset), /E.R. Degginger 13t (inset); Tony Stone Worldwide cover (main pic.); Wayland Picture Library 24(t), 25(b).
Running-head artwork by Kate Davenport. Artwork on pages 28-9 by Mark Whitchurch.